W9-BPM-464

An I Can Read Book®

WHO'S AFRAID OF THE DARK?

by Crosby Bonsall

HarperTrophy®
A Division of HarperCollins*Publishers*

Printed in the United States of America.
For information address HarperCollins Children's Books, a division
of HarperCollins Publishers, 10 East 53rd Street, New York, NY 10022.

Library of Congress Cataloging-in-Publication Data
Bonsall, Crosby Newell.
Who's afraid of the dark?

(An I can read book)
Summary: A small boy projects his fear of the
dark onto his dog.
[1. Night—Fiction.] I. Title.
PZ7.B64265Wi [E] 79-2700
ISBN 0-06-020598-9
ISBN 0-06-020599-7 (lib. bdg.)
ISBN 0-06-444071-0 (pbk.)

First Harper Trophy edition, 1985.

For Elie and Jack

Stella is afraid of the dark.

I have told her it is silly.

I have told her I will protect her.

But Stella is still scared.

When we go to bed she shivers.

In the dark she shakes.

She sees big scary shapes.

She hears little scary sounds.

She hears *ooohs* and *boooos*.

I tell her it is only the wind.

But Stella is still scared.

She hears steps on the roof.

I tell her it is only the rain.

But she hides anyway.

Stella is not very smart, is she?

Yes, she is too!

Stella sounds sort of silly to me.

She is not!

She must be.

She's afraid of the dark.

That is not silly!

YOU said it was.

That's right.

Well, Stella IS silly.

But YOU are not silly.
Why don't you teach Stella
not to be afraid of the dark?

How?

Hold her and hug her.

Hang on to her in the dark.

Let her know you are there.

Take care of her!

After a while she will know.

After a while

she won't need you anymore.

Not ever?

Only as a friend.

I will hold her

and hug her

tonight.

Don't be scared, Stella.

I will protect you.

I will take care of you.